Martians at
Mudpuddle Farm

Michael Morpurgo
and Shoo Rayner

Young Lions

Best Friends · Jessy Runs Away · **Rachel Anderson**
Changing Charlie · **Scoular Anderson**
Something Old · **Ruth Craft**
Weedy Me · **Sally Christie**
Almost Goodbye Guzzler · Two Hoots · **Helen Cresswell**
Magic Mash · Nina's Machines · **Peter Firmin**
Shadows on the Barn · **Sarah Garland**
Private Eye of New York · **Nigel Gray**
Clever Trevor · **Brough Girling**
The Thing-in-a-Box · **Diana Hendry**
Desperate for a Dog · Houdini Dog · **Rose Impey**
Georgie and the Dragon · **Julia Jarman**
Cowardy Cowardy Cutlass · Free With Every Pack ·
Mo and the Mummy Case · The Fizziness Business ·
Robin Kingsland
And Pigs Might Fly! · Albertine, Goose Queen · Jigger's Day Off ·
Martians at Mudpuddle Farm · Mossop's Last Chance ·
Michael Morpurgo
Hiccup Harry · Harry's Party · Harry with Spots On ·
Chris Powling
The Father Christmas Trap · **Margaret Stonborough**
Pesters of the West · **Lisa Taylor**
Jacko · Messages · Rhyming Russell · **Pat Thomson**
Monty, The Dog Who Wears Glasses · Monty Bites Back ·
Monty – Up To His Neck in Trouble · Monty Must be Magic ·
Colin West
Stone the Crows, It's a Vacuum cleaner ·
Ging Gang Goolie – It's An Alien! · **Bob Wilson**

For Eloise, her book

First published in Great Britain by
A & C Black (Publishers) Ltd 1992
First published in Young Lions 1993
10 9 8 7 6 5 4 3

Young Lions is an imprint of Collins Children's Books,
part of HarperCollins Publishers Ltd,
77–85 Fulham Palace Road, London W6 8JB

ISBN 0 00 674494 X

Printed and bound in Great Britain by HarperCollins Manufacturing, Glasgow

Chapter One

There was once a family of all sorts of animals that lived in the farmyard behind the tumble-down barn on Mudpuddle Farm.

WAKE UP YOU SLEEPY HEADS

At first light every morning Frederick, the flame-feathered cockerel, lifted his eyes to the sun and crowed and crowed until the light came on in old Farmer Rafferty's bedroom window.

One by one the animals crept out
into the dawn and stretched

and yawned

YAWNNNNNNN

and scratched themselves.

But no one ever spoke a word – not until after breakfast.

Early one morning old Farmer Rafferty looked out of his window. The corn was waving yellow in the sun. The stream ran clear and silver under the bridge, and the air was humming with summer.

The bees will be out flying today, and that means honey. And honey means money, and I need to buy a new tractor. The old one won't start in the mornings like it should. Get busy bees. Buzz my beauties, buzz!

Chapter Two

Deep in the beehive at the bottom
of the apple orchard, Little Bee was
getting ready for his first solo flight.

> Now remember,
> load up your pollen in the clover
> field, and then come straight
> home. And don't get lost. Good luck.

And off flew Little Bee out into the wide blue sky. Round and round he flew, looking for the clover field, but he couldn't find it anywhere.

So he buzzed down towards the old tractor where Mossop, the cat with the one and single eye, was trying hard not to wake up.

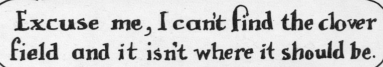

Mossop opened his eye.

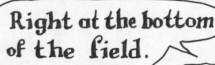

Then he went back to sleep again.

The trouble was that Little Bee
didn't know his right from his left
or his left from his right.

Round and round he flew

the Clover field,

flew looking for

to feel giddy

round and round till he began

Little Bee felt a great yawn coming on. He looked down for somewhere soft to sleep and then he saw the tractor with the old cat still asleep on the seat.

His tail looks nice and soft and warm. He won't mind, he won't even know I'm there.

And he was quite right about that.
Mossop never even felt Little Bee
land on his tail. He was too busy
dreaming. So Little Bee and Mossop
snoozed together in the sun and the
hours passed.

Chapter Three

Back in the beehive, Queen Bee
was getting worried. Little Bee had
been gone for hours now and
something had to be done.
She called all her bees together.

Right, forget pollen-gathering, forget honey-making. Little Bee is lost and we've got to find him before dark else he'll get cold and die. Follow me.

Ah-ha! Once more unto the breach!

Old Farmer Rafferty was milking
Aunty Grace, the dreamy-eyed
brown cow, when he heard the bees
coming. 'There they go,' he
chortled over his milk pail.

And then he began to sing as he often did when he was happy. He sang in a crusty, croaky kind of a voice, and he made it up as he went along.

Out in the clover field Diana the
silly sheep

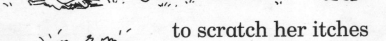

was rolling on her back

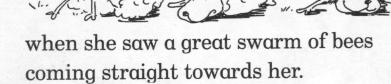

to scratch her itches

when she saw a great swarm of bees
coming straight towards her.

She struggled to her feet and ran off towards the pond as fast as her legs could carry her. No one was at all surprised when she jumped right in. That's what she always did when there were bees about.

As usual it was Jigger, the almost always sensible sheep dog, who had to pull her out.

Silly sheep!

They can't sting you in the water. That's what my mother told me.

'And some mothers do have them,' thought Albertine from her island in the pond.

It's just bees buzzing. Nothing to worry about.

That's my Mum!

She's so calm in a crisis!

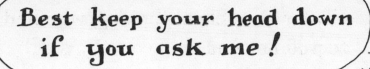

Best keep your head down if you ask me!

said
Upside
and Down.

So the two white ducks that no one could tell apart upside-downed themselves in the pond and stayed there all day long.

Captain, the great black carthorse who loved everyone and whom everyone loved, looked out over the clover field.

I don't like the look of this at all. There's too many of them and.... and they're coming this way!
Do pigs like honey, mummy?
I shouldn't be surprised if they do!

And sure enough, the sky above
them suddenly darkened and the
humming became a droning and
the droning became a roaring.

The bees were right over their heads now and they sounded angry, **very angry indeed!**

DON'T MOVE!

But no one could move anyway.
They were all too terrified, except
Albertine of course.

'Albertine,' said Captain without
moving his lips. 'What are we
going to do?'

Chapter Four

Albertine thought her deep goosey
thoughts for a moment. Then she
said, 'Just follow me'. And she
swam across the pond, waddled
through the open gate and out into
the cornfield beyond.

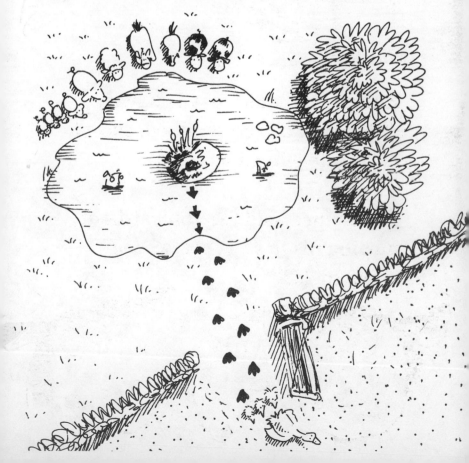

All the animals followed because they knew that Albertine was the most intelligent goose that ever lived. If anyone knew what to do, she would. They reached the middle of the cornfield and looked up. The bees were still following them.

Albertine began to run
round in a great big circle.

"All the animals did the same, running round and round"

"And above them the bees all flew round and round and round."

'I wish,' said Aunty Grace,

I wish someone would tell me why we're doing this. The bees aren't going away and I'm feeling giddy.

Me too dear!

said Primrose.

'Good,' said Albertine.

If you're feeling giddy, then the bees are feeling giddy.

She's so logical!

Not many people know this, but when a bee feels giddy, he gets sleepy too; and then he'll buzz off home to sleep. Never fails, you'll see. Keep going.

So round and round they all ran until suddenly the buzzing stopped. When they looked up the bees had all buzzed off, just as Albertine had said they would.

Chapter Five

The bees were flying home over the farmyard when one of them suddenly spotted Little Bee all curled up asleep on Mossop's tail. 'Follow me,' said Queen Bee and down they flew.

Yes Mo'am!

LITTLE BEE

'I got lost,' cried Little Bee.

'Soon,' Queen Bee yawned.
She could hardly keep her eyes
open, she was so sleepy.

And so that's what they all did.
Soon there was a great ball of
snoozing bees hanging on
Mossop's tail.

Back in the cornfield, Captain had
a worried look on his face.
'Just look what we've done to
Farmer Rafferty's corn,' he said.
'Just look.' And they looked.

They had flattened out a huge
circle in the corn. Not a single
solitary stalk still stood standing.

They all heard him. He was
walking into the field singing his
honey song.

Honey, oh honey. Won't you be

When Farmer Rafferty reached
the middle of the cornfield, there
wasn't an animal to be found.
What he did find was a great
circle of flattened corn.

CRIKEY!

ny hon

Well, I'll be jiggered! A perfect corn circle. I've heard about these. Maybe it's flying saucers, maybe it's Martians with ray guns.

And he began to chortle and his eyes began to twinkle.

Farmer Rafferty
danced a giggling
jig all around the corn
circle till he got
giddy and had
to sit down.

Then off he went towards the farmhouse, counting on his fingers and muttering to himself.

He didn't know it, but from behind the farmyard wall the animals were watching and listening to every word.

'What's a Martian?' Diana asked and of course everyone looked at Albertine.

'Well,' she said, thinking very hard indeed, 'they walk stiffly like robots do and they carry ray-guns like Farmer Rafferty says.' The animals could hardly believe it, but if Albertine had told them then it had to be true. After all there was nothing Albertine didn't know.

Chapter Six

Farmer Rafferty was still counting on his fingers when he passed by the old tractor and noticed the ball of bees hanging on Mossop's tail.

Oh dear me. My bees have gone and swarmed. Perhaps they couldn't find the way back home. I'll have to put them back in their hive.

And he disappeared inside the farmhouse.

While he was gone, the animals
crept back into the farmyard, just
in time to notice something coming
in through the farmyard gate.
It was dressed in white from
head to toe.

It wore a white helmet

and white gloves

and it walked stiffly like a robot,

and as it walked it puffed smoke
out of its ray-gun.

In its other hand it carried
a great big sack.

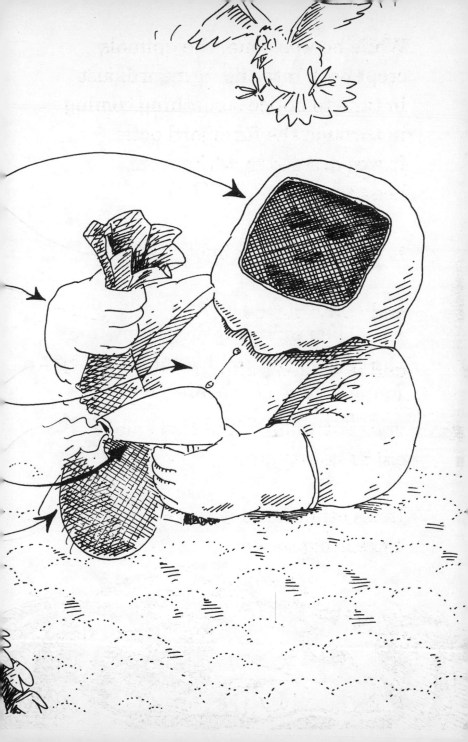

A Martian!

Diana cried. And she ran, they all ran. They ran until they came to the edge of the pond where they found Albertine washing herself.

'It's a Martian,' panted Jigger, the almost always sensible sheepdog.

Albertine smiled her goosey smile.

Look again.

That's not Martians, that's Old Farmer Rafferty in his bee-keeping costume. Now watch...

And they watched as old Farmer Rafferty puffed smoke around the swarm of bees.

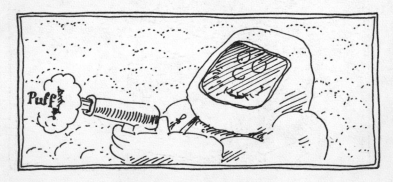

Farmer Rafferty scooped the bees into his sack, and off he went singing his honey song, with Queen Bee and Little Bee and all the others still snoozing inside.

Chapter Seven

Later that afternoon the first cars arrived. Before long, Front Meadow was filled hedge to hedge with cars, and there were people everywhere. Mossop, who had woken up by now, walked down the lane and met Jigger and the others.

CHILDREN'S CORNER ▶

TEAS ▶

Old Farmer Rafferty put up notices everywhere. I've eaten most of them.

KEEP OFF THE CORN!

◀ UP!

CUT FLOWERS

FRUIT ▶

DO NOT FEED THE ANIMALS!

VISITOR CENTRE ▶

TOM -A- TOES

Potatoes

It says...

RAFFERTY'S CORN CIRCLE
GENUINE
MARTIAN CORN CIRCLE

To visit .... Two Pounds

Car Park .... Two Pounds

Martian Cream Tea..... Two Pounds

(Honey <u>not</u> Strawberry Jam!)

'No one's going to believe a silly
story like that, are they?' said
Jigger; but when Albertine looked
at him he wished he hadn't said it.

'Course
not.

It's just
Stories.

I don't like
stories. You can't
eat them.

'I think,' said Albertine 'that we
believe mostly what we want to
believe.'

Deep thinking that.
What a clever
goose you are.

I Know.

She's so
wonderful!

Chapter Eight

That afternoon Farmer Rafferty
showed all the visitors round his
Martian corn circle.

After that they settled down on the
front lawn to a Martian cream tea.

He told them the story of the flying
saucer and the Martians that had
landed on Mudpuddle Farm, and
they swallowed it all (the cream
teas and the story) and went
home happy.

And old Farmer Rafferty was happy too. He'd soon have enough money to buy his new tractor.

All red and shiny it would be, with
a proper cab on it so he could
plough his fields without getting
wet and so Mossop could sleep out
of the wind.

But Mossop was quite happy out on the old tractor in the farmyard. None of the animals ever told him about the day the bees swarmed on his tail. They thought it might give him bad dreams, and they didn't want that.

The night came down, the moon came up, and everyone slept on Mudpuddle Farm.